That's the One!

Copyright © QED Publishing 2007

First published in the UK in 2007 by
QED Publishing
A Quarto Group company
226 City Road
London EC1V 2TT
www.qed-publishing.co.uk

Reprinted in 2008

A catalogue record for this book is
available from the British Library.

ISBN 978 1 84835 001 4

Written by Bernard Ashley
Edited by Clare Weaver
Designed by Alix Wood
Illustrated by Janee Trasler
Consultancy by Anne Faundez

Publisher Steve Evans
Creative Director Zeta Davies
Senior Editor Hannah Ray

Printed and bound in China

That's the One!

Bernard Ashley

Illustrated by Janee Trasler

QED Publishing

It was Friday and Billy's mum and dad had an invitation to a party. But the invitation had been held up in the post, and the party was the next night. So soon!

"I fancy something different to wear," said Billy's mum. "A new look!"
"Sorry, but I can't help you choose," Billy's dad said. "I've got to go to work."
Billy's eyes lit up.

I'll come! I'll help you choose – and I can spend my birthday money from Nan.

Good idea!

said Dad.

Billy's dad was a fitter at **Fast-Fix.**

Billy liked to sit in the office and watch his dad at work. But today, Billy had a job to do as well.

Mum drove them into town. Try It On was the best place to look for Mum's new clothes. "Something different!" she said.

First, Mum chose a pretty blouse and a leather skirt with tassels. She showed them to the shop assistant, went into the changing rooms – and out came a cowgirl, like in a western film!

"That's the one!" said Billy.
And it gave him an idea.
He could choose a cowboy
hat as his birthday present.

"I look like I've lost my horse," Mum said, shaking her head.

Next, she picked a short dress in black-and-white stripes.

She showed it to the shop assistant, went into the changing rooms – and out came a sporty girl footballer, like in the women's team in the park.

"That's the one!" said Billy.
And it gave him a different idea.
He could choose a football for himself.

But Mum shook her head.
"That's not a winner!"

Then, she chose a long, bright dress with patterns of exotic flowers. She showed it to the shop assistant, went into the changing rooms – and out came a girl from Jamaica.

"That's the one!" said Billy.
And it gave him another idea.

He could choose a steel drum as his present.

"It doesn't bang the drum for me," Mum said.
Now she chose a white silk blouse and
matching headscarf.

She showed them to the
shop assistant, in she went
– and out came a pirate, as
exciting as Captain Annie in
Billy's *Sea Fighters* book.

"That's the one!" said Billy.
And what about a pirate's
telescope for himself?

"Doesn't grab me," Mum said.
Her final choice was a pretty green top
with a wide, white collar, and matching tights.
She showed them to the shop assistant,
in she went for the last time – and out
came Robin Hood from the pantomime.

"That's the one!" said Billy.
Great – a bow and arrow as his present!

"Misses the target with me,"
Mum sighed.
So, they went to Jack and Jill's
to choose Billy's present.

Mum was
disappointed that
she hadn't found
anything to wear, but
Billy looked high and
low until he saw just
the thing –

a little red sports car.

Dad came in wearing his dirty dungarees.

How did you get on? Dad asked.

But suddenly,
Mum was giving Dad
a long, hard look.

Wait and see!

Billy frowned.
He didn't get it.
Not at all.

It was the party night and Dad was waiting to go.

Are you ready yet?
We're going to be late! he called up the stairs.

They heard the bedroom door open. Mum was coming! And she looked lovely.

Her necklace and her earrings sparkled, and so did her shiny, red shoes.

She couldn't have chosen anything more beautiful to wear than Dad's clean dungarees.

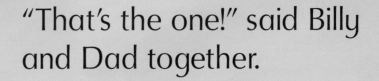

"That's the one!" said Billy and Dad together.

Notes for Teachers and Parents

- *That's the One!* is a realistic story that connects to Billy's fantasies. Talking and laughing about the pictures and the text helps involve the children in the book and develops reading and thinking skills.

- The story line offers opportunities to share stories of cowboys and pirates with the children. Do the children know what job cowboys and cowgirls used to do? 'Captain Annie' is a made-up pirate name. Have the children read any pirate stories or seen any pirate films? What were some of the pirates' names? Which pantomimes or Christmas shows have the children seen? Which characters were in them?

- Billy's dreams about football can lead to a discussion about the sport. What are the names of the children's favourite football teams? Can they name any of the players in the teams? Have any of the children been to watch a football match?

- Have any of the children ever taken part in a carnival or fancy-dress parade? What did they wear? Look out for news coverage of Caribbean carnivals as well as stories and books from and about the West Indies to show the children.

- Provide a dressing-up box for imaginative play. The children can act out the different characters in the story – for example, a mechanic at *Fast-Fix*, a football player or the clothes-shop assistant.

- Remember that play can lead to stories. Note down the children's stories, then write them on good paper (or on the computer) to make a special book for sharing. The children could illustrate the stories with their own drawings.

- Children are surrounded by text, indoors and out, and much of it can be useful in reading. How many words around them can the children read? Can they decode any words phonetically? Remember to keep everything light and fun, and stop when the children get bored or frustrated.

- The illustrations might inspire the children to think of new stories. For example, why is the woman in the background trying on hats? Can the children make up a story about her? When Billy is driving on the open road, where is he going – and where would the children like to go? Encourage the children to imagine what adventures could be had on the way.